D0241729

Stories to Share

Stories to Share

LITTLE TIGER PRESS
London

Contents

Follow That Bear If You DARE!

Claire Freedman

Alison Edgson

Hare loved bears.
He liked big bears, little bears,
hairy bears and scary bears.
   "If only I could find a bear,"
said Hare. "If only I could
catch one! The hairier and
scarier the better!"

So Hare bought a book:
The Best Book of Bear Hunting.
He opened his book
and took a look.

9

STEP 1

BEAR HUNTING

A WARNING
(please read carefully)

WHEN going on a hunt, to find a bear, you need to take the utmost care.

It's best to take a friend along too — choose one that looks much fatter than you!

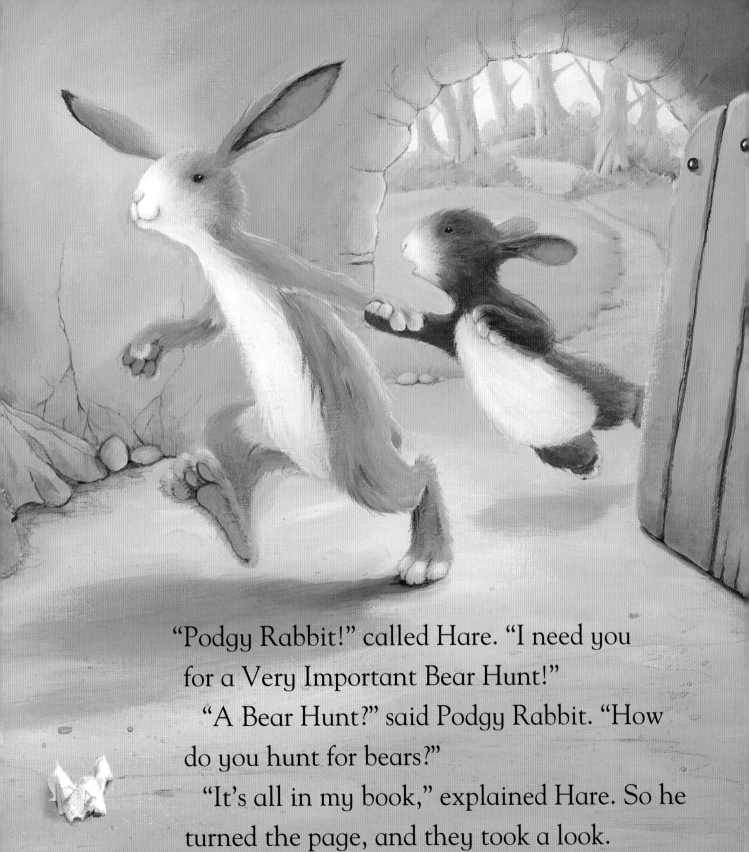

"Podgy Rabbit!" called Hare. "I need you
for a Very Important Bear Hunt!"

"A Bear Hunt?" said Podgy Rabbit. "How
do you hunt for bears?"

"It's all in my book," explained Hare. So he
turned the page, and they took a look.

THINGS YOU WILL NEED

*T*O catch your bear,

take a fishing net,

some string — as long as

you can get —

	L	S	D
~~	20	0	0
~~	10	5	2
~~	0	2	4
~~	30	7	6

A TORCH to shine
deep inside his lair,
and watchful eyes ~

BEARS LURK EVERYWHERE!

"Are you sure you want to find a bear, Hare?" said Podgy Rabbit.

"Of course!" Hare said. "The hairier and scarier the better! Look, I've found a fishing net, a torch and a piece of string. What's next?"

They turned another page in Hare's book and took a look.

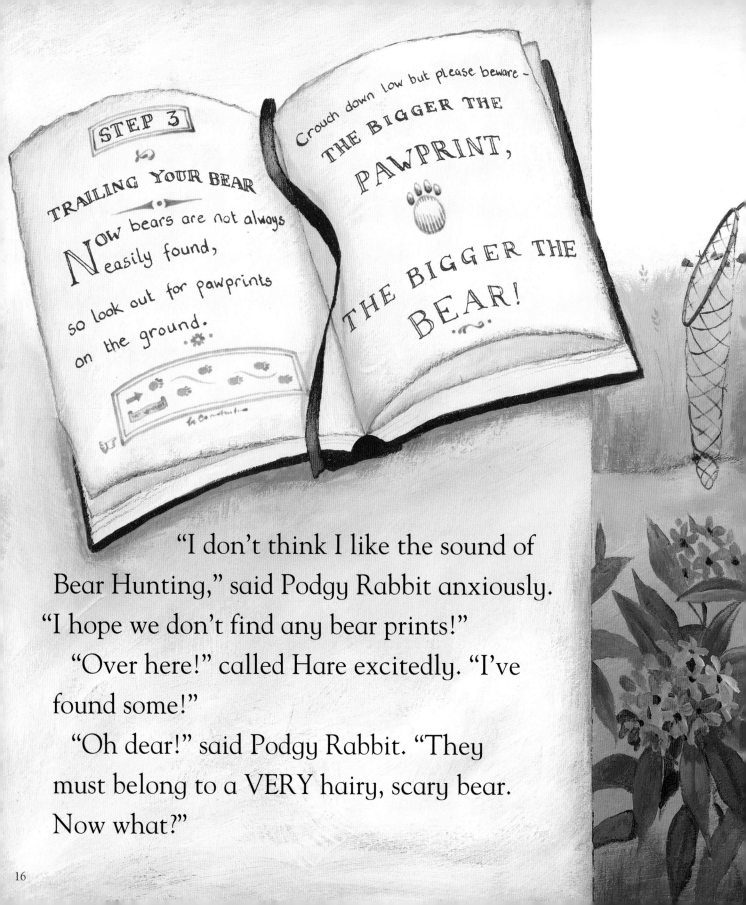

STEP 3

TRAILING YOUR BEAR

Now bears are not always easily found, so look out for pawprints on the ground.

Crouch down low but please beware —

THE BIGGER THE PAWPRINT, THE BIGGER THE BEAR!

"I don't think I like the sound of Bear Hunting," said Podgy Rabbit anxiously. "I hope we don't find any bear prints!"

"Over here!" called Hare excitedly. "I've found some!"

"Oh dear!" said Podgy Rabbit. "They must belong to a VERY hairy, scary bear. Now what?"

They turned another page of
Hare's book and took a look.

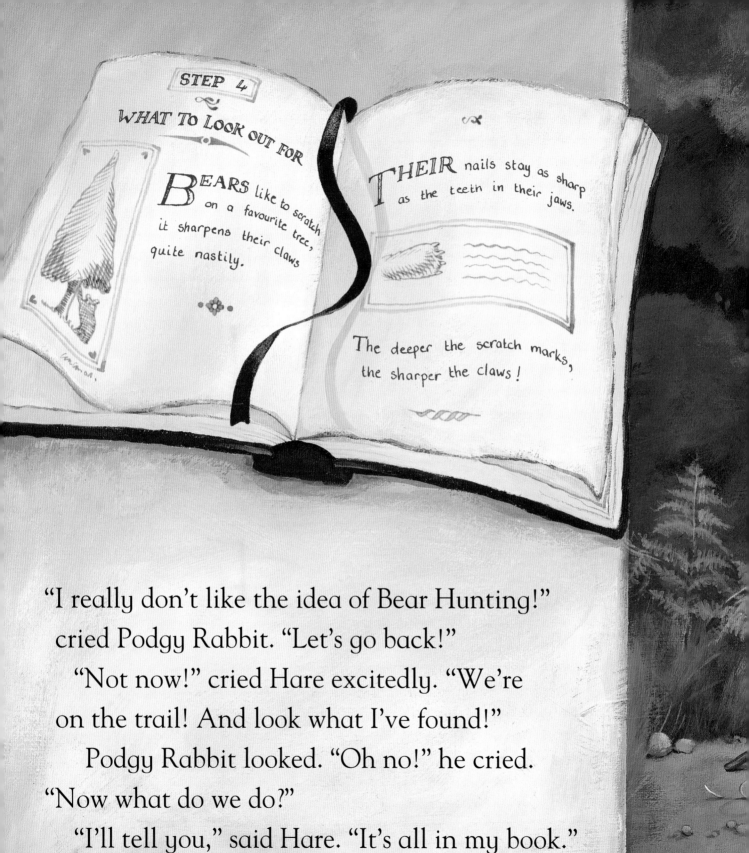

STEP 4

WHAT TO LOOK OUT FOR

BEARS like to scratch on a favourite tree, it sharpens their claws quite nastily.

THEIR nails stay as sharp as the teeth in their jaws.

The deeper the scratch marks, the sharper the claws!

"I really don't like the idea of Bear Hunting!" cried Podgy Rabbit. "Let's go back!"

"Not now!" cried Hare excitedly. "We're on the trail! And look what I've found!"

Podgy Rabbit looked. "Oh no!" he cried. "Now what do we do?"

"I'll tell you," said Hare. "It's all in my book."

So they turned another
page and took a look.

19

GETTING CLOSER AND CLOSER

WHEN a bear is close, you may hear grumbling, that is the sound of his tummy rumbling.

HIDE yourself quickly
and take great care —

the louder the rumble,
the hungrier the bear!

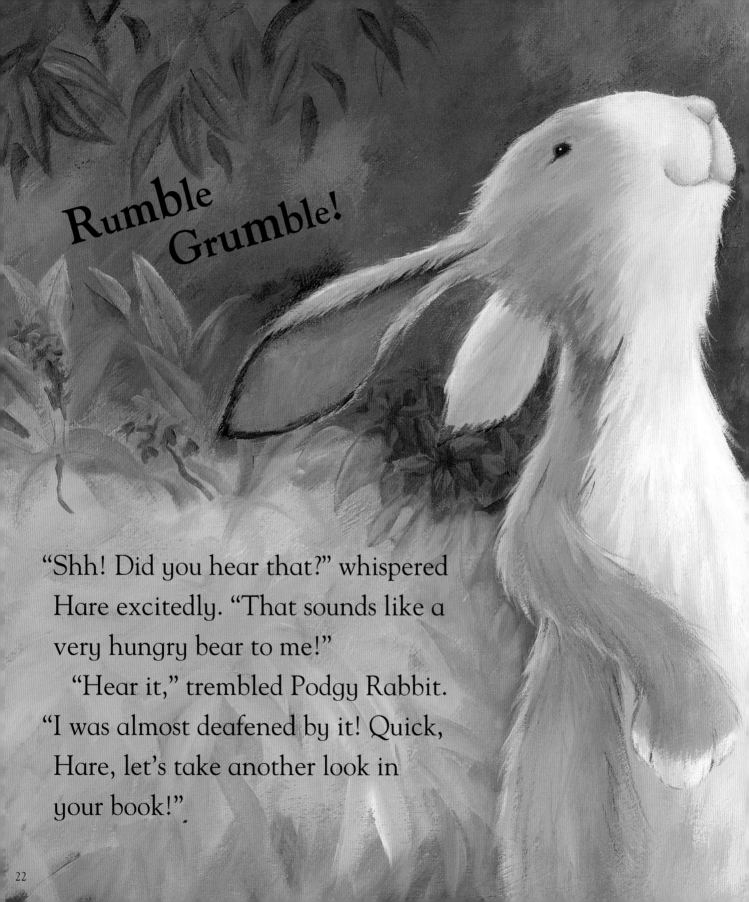

Rumble Grumble!

"Shh! Did you hear that?" whispered
Hare excitedly. "That sounds like a
very hungry bear to me!"

"Hear it," trembled Podgy Rabbit.
"I was almost deafened by it! Quick,
Hare, let's take another look in
your book!"

STEP 6

MEETING YOUR BEAR

MEETING your bear
can be quite shocking,
don't let him see
your knees are knocking.

SUCK in your tummy
and try to look thinner,
and hope that he's already
eaten his dinner!

"Yikes!" gulped Podgy Rabbit. "Look over there, Hare!"

"Where?"

"It's a BEAR!"

"HELP! We'll never catch HIM with a fishing net and a piece of string!" trembled Podgy Rabbit.

"Just watch me try!" cried Hare.

"I'm HUNGRY!" growled the bear.

Then, suddenly . . .

"Dinner's ready," called Mummy Bear.

"It's bear-sized beans on bear-sized toast."

"Yummy!" said Little Bear. "Must go!"

"Come back!" called Hare.
Poor Podgy Rabbit was too weak to speak!
"Oh no," cried Hare. "I can't lose
my bear – that's not fair!"

Quickly he took another look in his book.

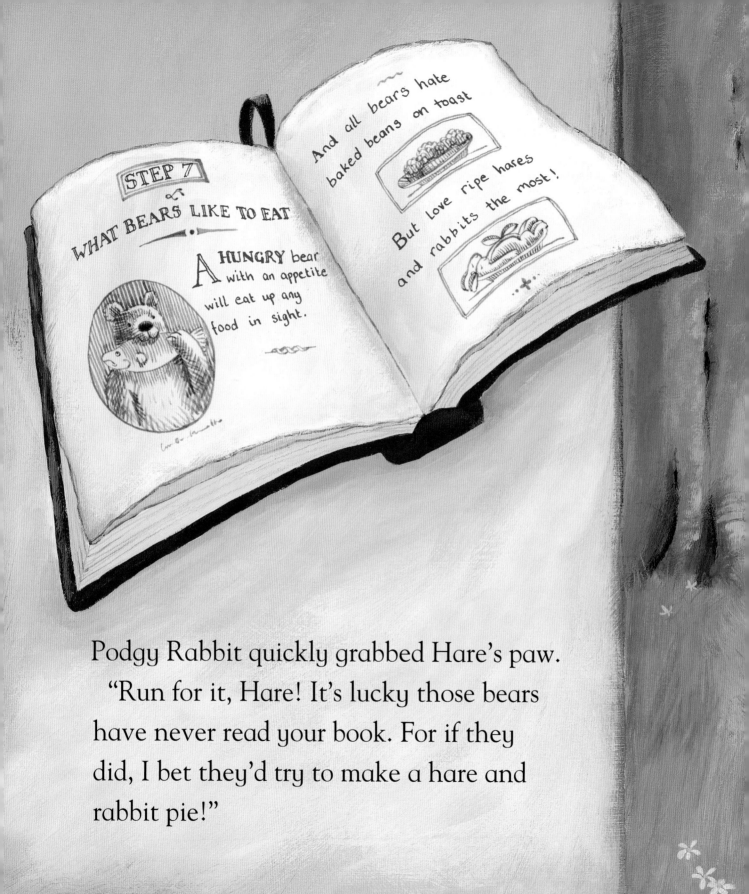

STEP 7

WHAT BEARS LIKE TO EAT

A HUNGRY bear with an appetite will eat up any food in sight.

And all bears hate baked beans on toast

But love ripe hares and rabbits the most!

Podgy Rabbit quickly grabbed Hare's paw. "Run for it, Hare! It's lucky those bears have never read your book. For if they did, I bet they'd try to make a hare and rabbit pie!"

Little Mouse and the Big Red Apple

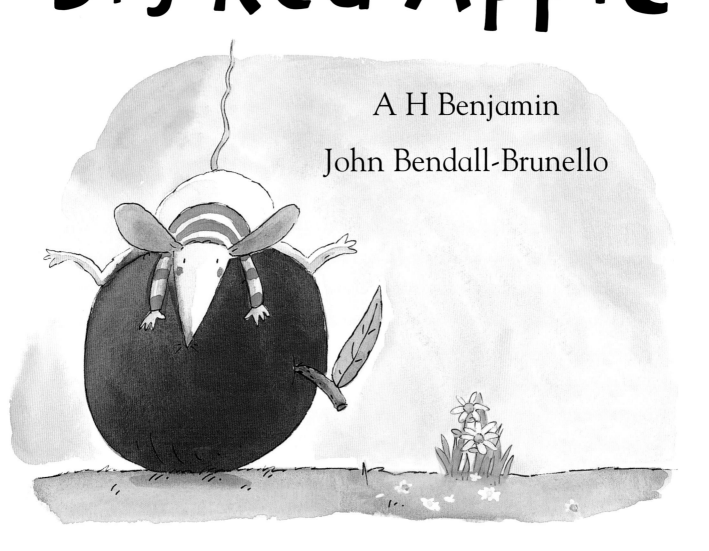

A H Benjamin

John Bendall-Brunello

Mouse was feeling a bit peckish
one day, when all of a sudden he
came across a big, red, juicy apple.
"Just what I fancy!" he cried.
"I'll take it home with me and have
a feast!"

Mouse set off towards his little house,
rolling the apple over and over.

He couldn't wait to get his teeth into
the big, red, juicy apple. "Yum, yum,"
he thought, when all of a sudden . . .

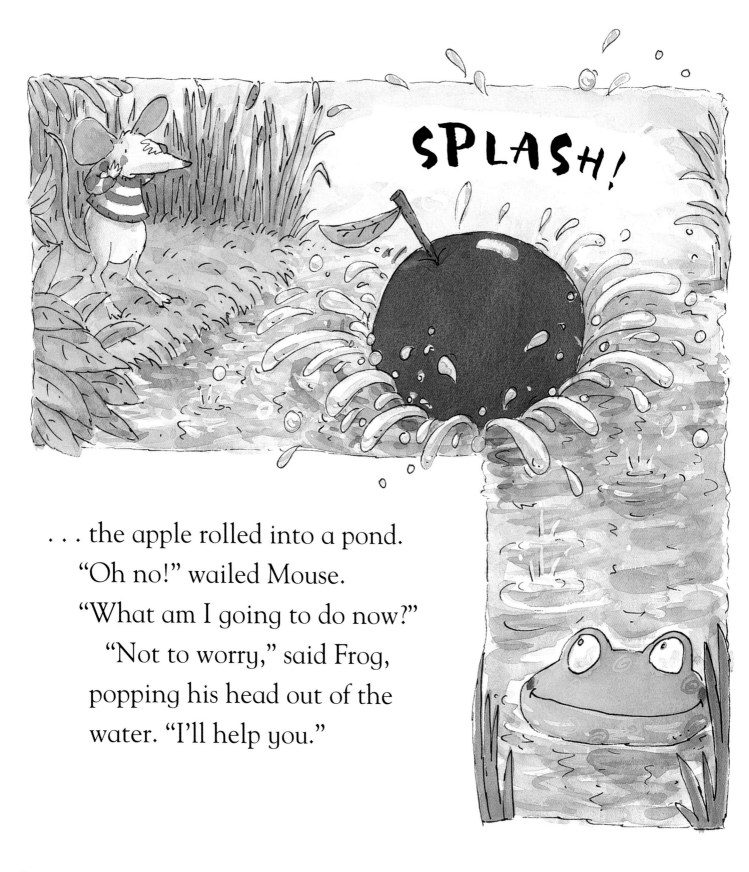

SPLASH!

. . . the apple rolled into a pond.

"Oh no!" wailed Mouse.

"What am I going to do now?"

"Not to worry," said Frog,
popping his head out of the
water. "I'll help you."

Frog kicked the apple hard
with his strong back legs.
It flew out of the water and. . .

BUMP!

. . . landed on the ground.
"There you are," said Frog.
He licked his lips and
stared at the apple.

"Er, thanks," said Mouse, as he began to roll it along the path. He did not want to share his apple with Frog. Mouse went on his way, thinking of the lovely apple dinner he would have later. His mouth was already watering when . . .

CRASH!

. . . the big, red, juicy apple fell into a thorn bush.

"Silly me!" muttered Mouse, as he tried to rescue his dinner. "Ouch, that hurt!" he cried. "Those prickles are nasty!"

"I see you have a problem," said Tortoise,
moving next to Mouse. "Leave it to me."
Tortoise didn't have to worry about
the sharp prickles. He had his shell
to protect him.

Without any trouble
at all, Tortoise crept
under the thorn bush and
brought out the big, red, juicy apple.
"Problem solved!" he said, stroking
the apple longingly.

"I'm ever so grateful," said
Mouse in a hurried voice, and he
was off again. He did not want to
share his apple with Tortoise.
"I'll soon be home and biting
into that big, red, juicy apple,"
thought Mouse, when . . .

. . . the apple rolled into a log.
  "That's all I need!" sighed Mouse when
  he saw that the log blocked his path.
  "How do I get round that?"

"Easy!" said Mole,
popping out of a
nearby hole. "I'll dig
you a tunnel."

And she did. She dug a
tunnel that went right
under the log.

47

It was just wide enough for Mouse
and the apple to go through it.

"Always glad to help!" said Mole, sniffing at
the big, red, juicy apple with her little nose.
    "It's very kind of you," said Mouse, and he
went on his way as fast as he could. He did
not want to share the apple with Mole.
    He rolled the apple over and over until . . .

. . . he came
to a steep hill.
His house was at
the very top.

PUSH

Push, push,
heave, heave,
went Mouse,
grunting and
groaning.

PUSH

Up, up, up
he went,
until he reached
the very top.

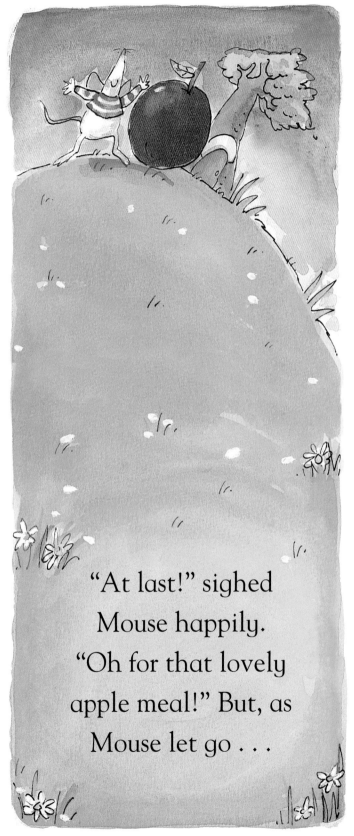

"At last!" sighed
Mouse happily.
"Oh for that lovely
apple meal!" But, as
Mouse let go . . .

. . . the apple wobbled,
and then it started
to roll . . .

down the
other side
of the hill!

It rolled
faster and
faster…

further
and further,
until…

. . . it came to a stop at the bottom
of the hill. Mouse could see
it lying there, like a big,
red jewel.

"Oh no," he cried,
"I'll have to start
all over again!"

54

Mouse scrabbled down the hill on his little
tired feet. Faster and faster he ran . . .

. . . but when he reached the bottom he found Frog, Mole and Tortoise had got there first!

"How kind of you to send that apple all the way back to us," called out Mole, chomping away on a piece of it.

Mouse gave a big, big sigh. "Don't mention it," he said. "Isn't that what friends are for?"

The Nutty Nut Chase

Kathryn White • Vanessa Cabban

Hickory was making rude faces at Pecan when the strangest thing happened.

POP!

A shiny brown nut suddenly
burst up from the ground. It
wobbled and shook, wibbled
and quivered, then lay there,
teasingly delicious.

63

"Wow, lunch!" Pecan shouted.

"Wow, lunch and dinner!" Hickory screeched.

"It's my nut," said Pecan.

"It's mine!" snapped Hickory.

"Who's making that noise?" shouted Badger.
"I'm trying to sleep."
    All the animals came out to see what
was happening.

"My nut!" Pecan shouted.

"It's mine!" yelled Hickory. "I saw it first."

"Did not."

"Did so."

"Box his ears!" shouted Littlest Rabbit.

"Certainly not. Boxing ears doesn't solve problems," said Badger firmly.

"Oh," said Littlest Rabbit, disappointed, "then bop his nose."

"No boxing or bopping,"
said Badger. "There will
be a competition and the
winner will get the nut."

"I know," said Hedgehog. "The prickliest wins the nut."

"But you're the prickliest," said Pecan and Hickory.

"So I am!" said Hedgehog, delighted. "I win! I get the nut."

"Cuddliest gets the nut," said Littlest Rabbit, "I win!"

"Enough!"
said Badger. "We will have a
race. First to reach the post wins."
    "Hooray, a race!" everyone cheered.

Blackbird whistled the
start of the race. They were off!
  Pecan and Hickory shot ahead
but the rabbits were close behind.
Hedgehog tried to run but only managed
a waddle. In a huff, he curled himself into
a ball and rolled full speed down the slope.
  Littlest Rabbit looked back to see a prickly
ball spinning towards them. "Look out!"
he called. But it was too late!

Hedgehog crashed through
the racers like a cannonball
and everyone landed in a
prickly heap.

"Oh dear," tutted Badger.
"We'll have to start again.
And prickly cannonballs
aren't allowed."

Hedgehog snorted
and sulked off.

Blackbird whistled and they were off again.

Pecan and Hickory were neck and neck.

"My nut!" shouted Pecan triumphantly. "I win!"

"No!" shouted Hickory. "It's mine! I win!"

Suddenly the nut began to move. It twitched and jerked, joggled and jiggled until PLOP! it disappeared down under the ground.

"It's a magic nut!" shouted Littlest Rabbit.

"Nutty magic!" squealed Hedgehog, racing back to see.

"Bet it would have tasted magic too," said Shrew.

POP!

The nut sprang up
right in front of Shrew.

"Quick, grab it!" shouted Littlest Rabbit.

All the animals shot across the grass, rolling
and shrieking, jumping and hopping, banging and
bopping into each other.

"I've got it!" shouted Hedgehog, but the nut
vanished again.

"That's my nose!" Shrew squeaked.

"Shhhhh!" said Badger suddenly. "Look."

He pointed at the magic nut that had appeared at his feet. Everyone tiptoed up to it. The nut shook and quivered. The animals looked in amazement.

"Help!" squealed the nut.

"AAAH!" shrieked Littlest Rabbit. "A talking nut."

"You're a talking nut," said Pecan.

Pecan and Hickory bent down and pulled and tugged, yanked and wrenched at the nut with all their might.

Out flew the nutshell, sending Pecan and
Hickory rolling backwards. And there,
where the nut had been, was Mole!

POP!

Mole shook himself and stood up on his two tiny legs. "Thanks!" he said. "I thought I would be stuck in that nutshell for ever."

Littlest Rabbit put the empty shell on his head. "It makes a great hat," he giggled.

"That looked like the tastiest nut ever," groaned Pecan and Hickory.

"There's plenty more where that came from," chirped Mole and he disappeared underground.

Suddenly shiny nuts began popping
up all over the place.

"There's enough for everyone!"
Mole chuckled.

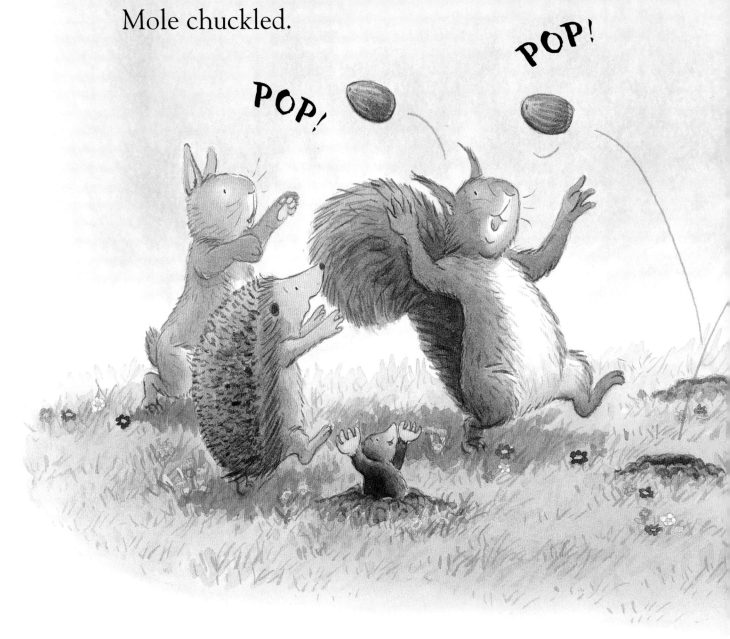

"Magic!" shouted Hickory.
"Magic!" shouted Pecan.
"Nutty magic!" everyone shouted,
and they all munched with delight.

POP!

POP!

YUCK!
That's not a Monster!

Angela McAllister • Alison Edgson

Mr and Mrs Monster were very
proud of their three eggs.
Mr Monster kept them warm by
huffing with his hot, stinky breath.
Mrs Monster screeched to them.

One stormy night,
the first egg cracked.
Out climbed an ugly little
monster, with prickly spikes
and snarly fangs.
"Aaah! He's FRIGHTFUL!"
sighed Mr and
Mrs Monster happily.
So that's what they
called him.

Then the second
egg cracked. Out climbed another
ugly little monster, with horny
spines and bristly warts.
"Oooh! She's HORRID!"
gasped Mr and Mrs Monster
happily. So that's what
they called her.

Then the third egg shook a bit. Frightful
and Horrid gave it a poke. Out crept
something very soft and pink.
"UGH! HE'S SWEET!!"
said the little monsters.
"LET'S SQUASH HIM!"

"Well, he's not what we expected," said Mrs Monster. "He is a bit of a shock."

"Let's throw him in the rubbish bin," said Mr Monster.

Suddenly there was a crash of thunder.

"Mama!" cried the fluffy
one and jumped into Mrs
Monster's arms.

She looked down at her
bundle of sweetness. "I think
we'll keep him," she said. "He
may look different but inside
he is a monster, just like us."

So they called him
Little Shock.

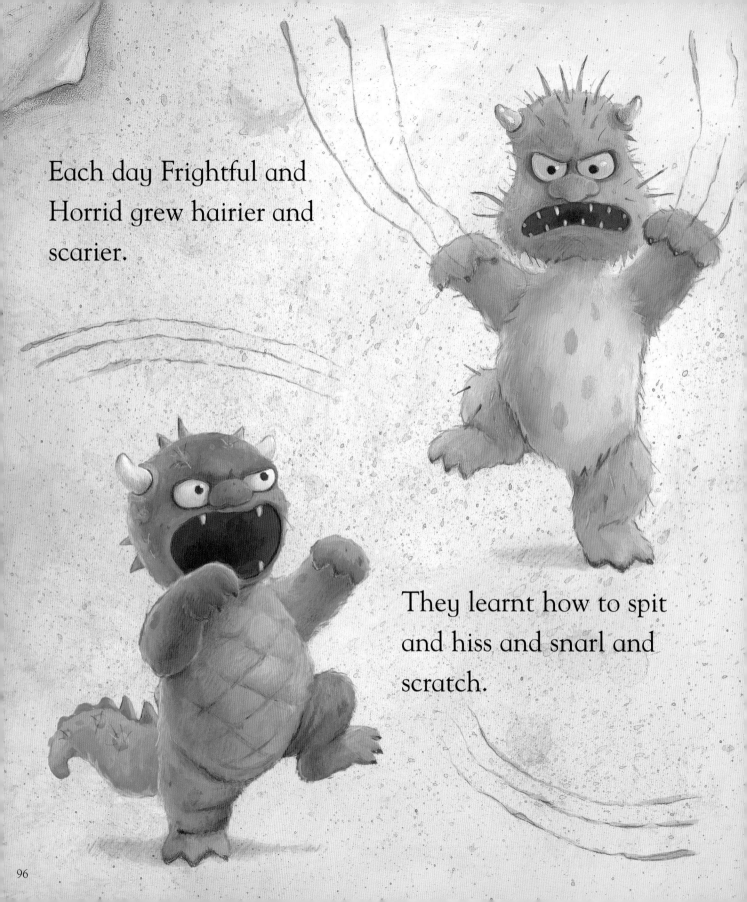

Each day Frightful and Horrid grew hairier and scarier.

They learnt how to spit and hiss and snarl and scratch.

But Little Shock grew MORE
fluffy. He liked to gurgle and roly-poly
and twinkle his big blue eyes. He loved
his brother and sister and followed
them everywhere.

AWOOOOOOOOOOOO!

"If you want to play with us you've got to be wild
and rampageous," said Frightful and Horrid.
    They showed him how to howl at the moon
until it hid behind a cloud. But Little Shock
was afraid of the dark.

They showed him how to squash and stamp
and trample. But Little Shock saw a worried
worm and sat down to give it a hug.

"Ugh!" sneered Frightful and Horrid.
"He's just a cutie-pie!"

Soon Frightful and Horrid were bold
enough to go monstering in the wood.

"You must take your brother with you,"
insisted Mrs Monster.

Frightful and Horrid snorted grumpily
but they put Little Shock in a trolley, hid
him under a blanket and tugged him along.

In the wood, Frightful leapt out at
a fox and made its fur turn white.
Horrid pounced on a wild pig and
made it jump into a tree.
They had a wonderful time!

GRRR!

RARGH!

Little Shock cuddled his blanket
and played peek-a-boo with a mouse.

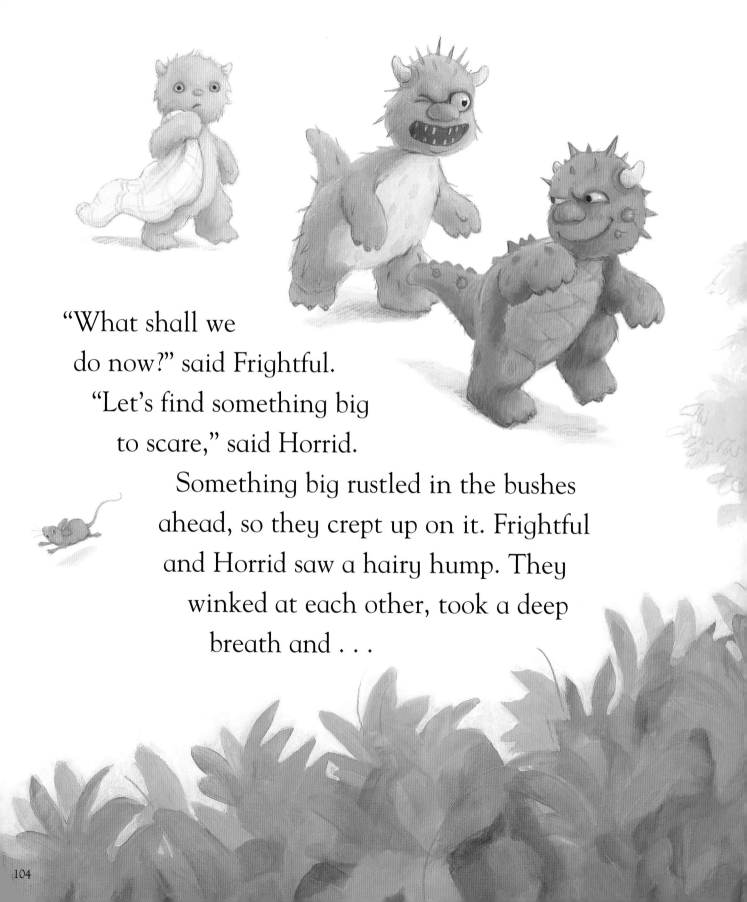

"What shall we
do now?" said Frightful.
"Let's find something big
to scare," said Horrid.
Something big rustled in the bushes
ahead, so they crept up on it. Frightful
and Horrid saw a hairy hump. They
winked at each other, took a deep
breath and . . .

But the hairy hump was only a little bit of a BIG monster! It snarled and flashed its fiery eyes. "WHO DARED TO ROAR AT ME?"

Frightful and Horrid were
too terrified to run away.
Their spines shrivelled
and their claws curled up.

Suddenly the BIG monster
spotted Little Shock.

"OOOH! CANDYFLOSS!"
he said.

Little Shock stared up at
the monster's face. His big
blue eyes grew wider
and wider . . .

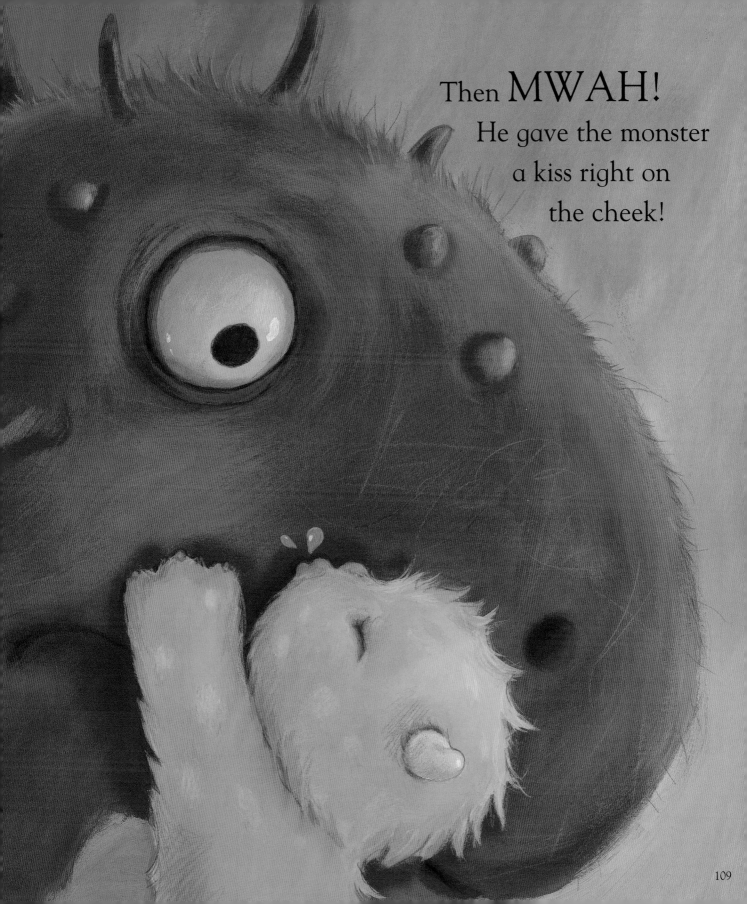

Then MWAH!
He gave the monster
a kiss right on
the cheek!

109

"YEUCH!"

The BIG monster wailed and dropped Little Shock in horror. He was so afraid that his fur turned to frizz and his bristles fell out.

"HELP!" he cried. "IT'S ADORABLE!"

And he ran away, crying for his mummy.

Frightful and Horrid couldn't believe their eyes.

"You kissed him! You kissed him!" they laughed.

Horrid swung her little brother high in the air and sat him on Frightful's shoulders.

"Maybe being cute could be useful after all," she said, giving him a pinch.

Little Shock just purred happily.

"Come on, then," said Frightful proudly, "let's go home and ALL kiss Mum and Dad!"

The Little
Lost Robin

Elizabeth Baguley • Tina Macnaughton

On the edge of the deep wood lived an old hare. Once, he had leapt and pranced under the magical moon, but time had made him grey and stiff, and he no longer danced. Instead he spent his time looking out over the world, gently daydreaming.

Every day, Hare went to feed the small
brown birds, who chattered and chirruped.
Remembering his long-ago moondancing,
Hare tapped a merry paw to their busy tunes.
   One morning, in swooped a bird with
a berry-bright breast. "You're a bold little
robin," laughed Hare.

Even when autumn came, Hare still went
to share food with his friends. But then
a chill wind scattered the leaves, and the
birds, too cold to stay, flew far away.
    Their song echoed with goodbye.
    "I'll miss you, little birds," sighed Hare.

Then something made Hare prick up his ears.
A song! A song that lilted faintly, away in
the wood. It was a bird! Hare hurried towards
the fir tree where Robin shone scarlet, singing
a song warm as summer.

"Robin! You didn't fly away!" exclaimed Hare.

And as Robin sang brightly, Hare wound round in a slow dance.

"You've made this old hare feel young again," he laughed.

So, every day, Hare would walk into the blustery woods to bring Robin seeds and sway to her song.

When winter arrived, freezing the wood and stiffening Hare's legs, Robin would come to the burrow to see him. Hare would wake as soon as the sun rose, and wait for her so that they could eat breakfast together.

"What would I do without you?" smiled Hare.

Then came a night that howled with storm-fury.
A wild wind exploded into the wood, blasting and
splintering trees. In whirled the snow, hiding the
land under its biting cold whiteness.

Deep in his burrow, Hare could not sleep
for worry about Robin. Had she been blown
into the storm, homeless and afraid?

At first light Hare rushed outside, hoping that Robin would be waiting for him. But there was no Robin, no Robin anywhere! Where was she? Why hadn't she come? Hare had to try to find her.

Out into the snowy wood
Hare struggled. Finally he
came to Robin's tree and
stopped. It lay fallen, wrenched
from the ground by the storm.
"Robin!" he gasped. "Where are you?"
But, searching through the
branches, Hare found only
her empty nest.

He slumped down, sure
that Robin was lost.

Just then, a tiny cheep made
him look up.

"Robin!" Hare shouted in
amazement. "I thought the
storm had taken you!"

As fast as she could, Robin flew to him.

"It's all right, little one," Hare said gently. "You can come back with me. I'll plant your tree outside my burrow, so you'll be quite at home."

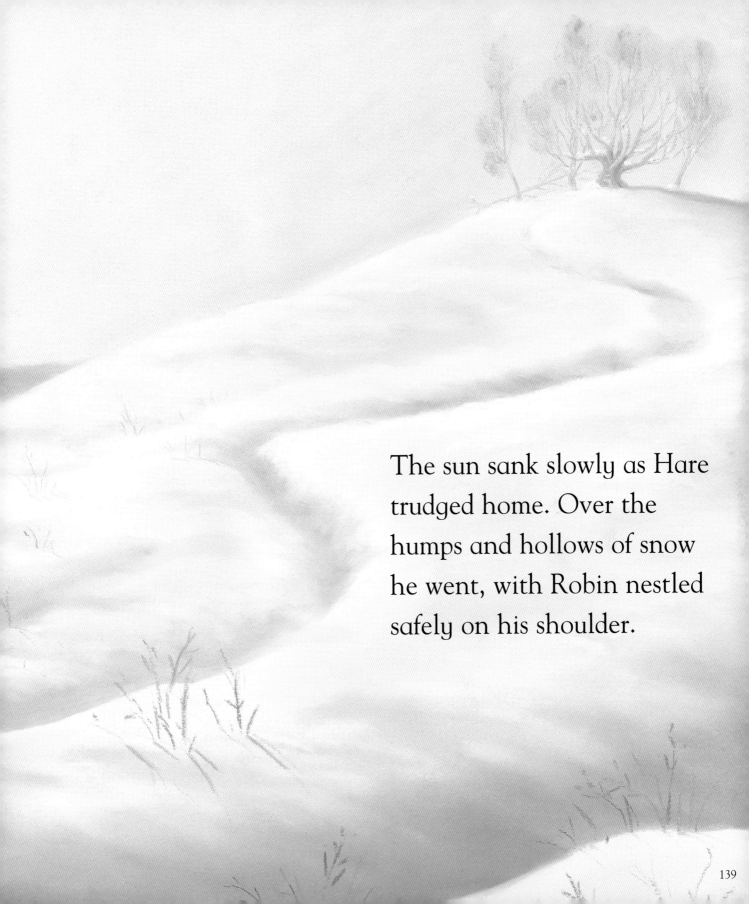

The sun sank slowly as Hare trudged home. Over the humps and hollows of snow he went, with Robin nestled safely on his shoulder.

Back home, Hare helped Robin make a new nest in the fir tree's branches. Every day she warbled and whistled, and when the night brought the light of the magical moon, Hare joyfully danced to her winter-bright tunes.

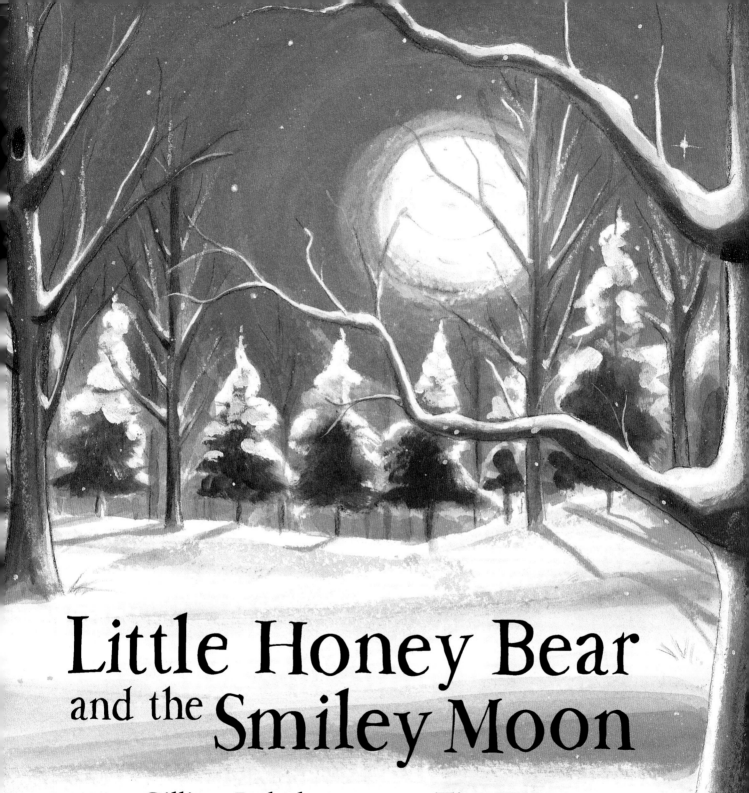

Little Honey Bear
and the Smiley Moon

Gillian Lobel   Tim Warnes

Little Honey Bear couldn't sleep.
Through his bedroom window the
moon was shining, as bright as day.
The snowy woods glimmered in
the brilliant moonlight. And surely
the moon was smiling at him!

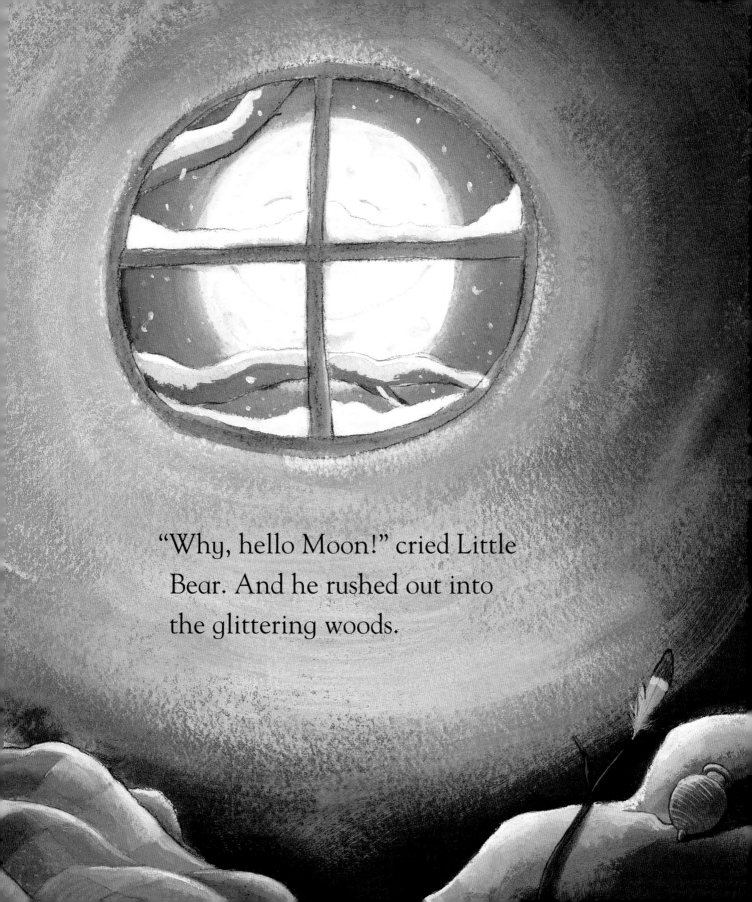

"Why, hello Moon!" cried Little Bear. And he rushed out into the glittering woods.

There in the moonlight was Lily Long Ears, making snow hares.

"Hello, Little Honey Bear," said Lily. "Couldn't you sleep either?"

"Oh Lily," said Little Bear, "the moon sailed right in front of my window, and she smiled at me!"

"Me too!" said Lily. "She's so big and smiley tonight, I just had to come out to say hello."

She showered Little Bear with snow. "Catch me if you can!" she cried, and darted away through the trees.

149

They ran through the moonlit
woods into a wide snowy meadow.
High above hung the moon and
right across the frozen meadow
ran a shining silver pathway.

"It's a pathway to the moon!"
cried Little Bear. "Just think, Lily –
we could walk all the way to the
moon and say hello."

"Little Honey Bear," squeaked
a tiny voice. "Can I come too?"

"'Course you can, Teeny Tiny
Mouse," said Little Bear.

So off along the moonpath
went the three friends.

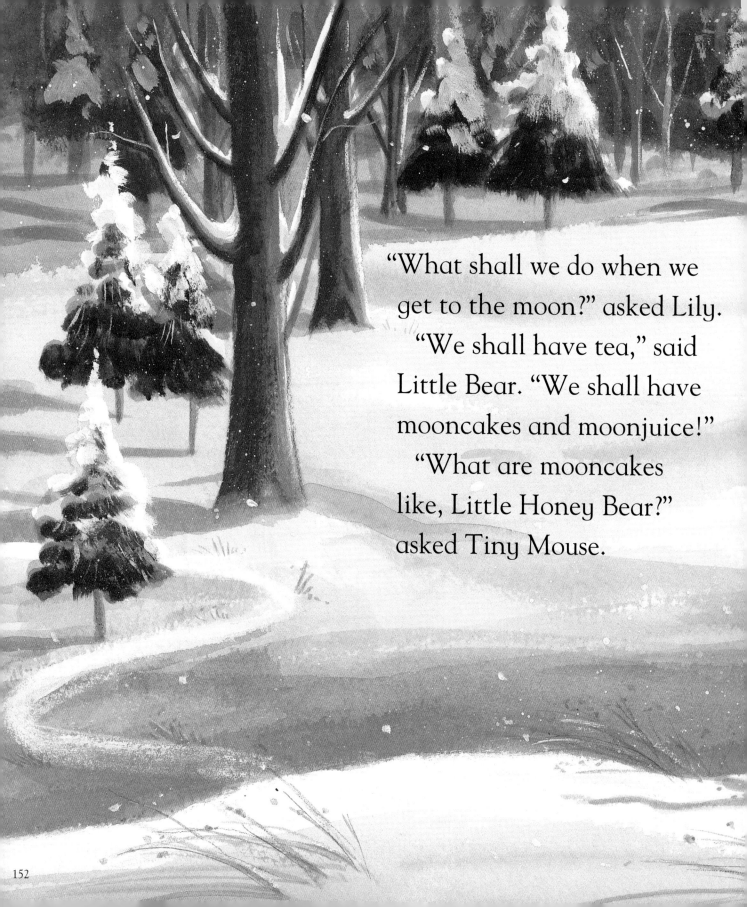

"What shall we do when we get to the moon?" asked Lily.

"We shall have tea," said Little Bear. "We shall have mooncakes and moonjuice!"

"What are mooncakes like, Little Honey Bear?" asked Tiny Mouse.

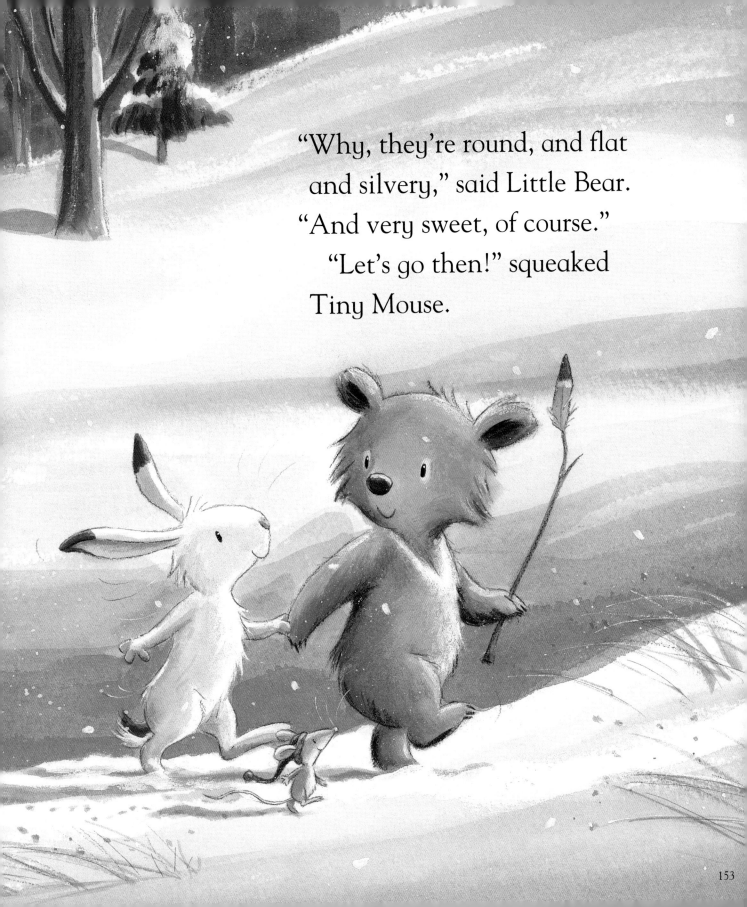

"Why, they're round, and flat and silvery," said Little Bear. "And very sweet, of course."

"Let's go then!" squeaked Tiny Mouse.

Suddenly the night grew colder.
A crisp wind whipped the snow
into little flurries. The path to the
moon grew steeper and steeper.

"It's an awful long way to
the moon," gasped Tiny Mouse.
"My little paws are freezing."

So Little Bear scooped Tiny
Mouse into his paw, and set him
on his big shoulder.

"That's much better!" said
Tiny Mouse, tucking his toes
into Little Bear's thick furry coat.
"My paws are happy now."

Up and up ran the moonpath towards
the very top of the hill. Snowflakes stung
their eyes and whirled into their ears.

"Do you think we'll get there soon,
Little Honey Bear?" gasped Lily.
"Only my ears are getting rather cold!"
As she spoke a great cloud blew in
front of the moon . . .

. . . and the moonpath disappeared. Suddenly it was very dark.

"I don't like it, Little Honey Bear," said Lily. "I don't like it at all!"

"I d-d-don't think I want to go to the moon after all," said Tiny Mouse. "Even for mooncakes."

So off they set down the hill.

Down and down they slipped and slithered, until they reached the woods.

"Perhaps the moon is cross and doesn't want to see us after all," said Little Honey Bear.

"I want to go home," quavered Tiny Mouse.

"Me too!" gasped Lily.

But everything looked
different in the dark,
and they couldn't find
their way home.

The trees creaked and
groaned, and the wood
was full of shadows.
   "I think we're lost,"
sniffed Little Bear. "And
I want my mummy!"

Suddenly a silvery light
flooded the woods. And
up above, bobbing between
the trees, the smiling moon
appeared.

"Hooray!" cried everyone.
And then the moonlight
fell upon a big furry bear,
her arms open wide as she
ran towards them.

"Oh Little Honey Bear,
I'm so glad I've found you!"
cried Mummy Bear. And
she gave them all a very
big bear hug.

"Oh Mummy," said Little Bear. "We were going to have tea with the moon, but then she got cross with us, and hid."

"And we didn't get to drink moonjuice," sighed Tiny Mouse.

"Or taste mooncakes," said Lily sadly.

Mother Bear smiled as she took them all back to the warm bear house for a special moon supper, with golden honey cakes and warm milk to drink.

"The moon wasn't cross. She was there all along," she said, "only the clouds were hiding her!"

"Mummy," said Little Bear later,
as she tucked him up in his bed,
"I did so very much want to go
and see the moon."
   "Why, Little Bear, we
don't need to go to the moon
to see her – she's all around us!"

168

Little Honey Bear looked through the window. Every tree was hung with a thousand glassy rainbows in the bright moonlight. And then the moon sailed through the trees and smiled at him.

"Goodnight, Moon," said Little Bear, rubbing his eyes. Then he turned over and fell fast asleep.

STORIES TO SHARE

LITTLE TIGER PRESS
1 The Coda Centre
189 Munster Road, London SW6 6AW
www.littletiger.co.uk

First published in Great Britain 2014

This volume copyright © Little Tiger Press 2014
Cover artwork copyright © Tim Warnes 2006,
Gwyneth Williamson 2000, Alison Edgson 2007
All rights reserved

Printed in China
LTP/1800/0982/0914
ISBN 978-1-84895-957-6
2 4 6 8 10 9 7 5 3 1

FOLLOW THAT BEAR IF YOU DARE!

Claire Freedman
Illustrated by Alison Edgson

First published in Great Britain 2007
by Little Tiger Press

Text copyright © Claire Freedman 2007
Illustrations copyright © Alison Edgson 2007

LITTLE MOUSE AND THE BIG RED APPLE

A H Benjamin
Illustrated by Gwyneth Williamson

First published in Great Britain 2000
by Little Tiger Press

Text copyright © A H Benjamin 2000
Illustrations copyright © Gwyneth Williamson 2000

THE NUTTY NUT CHASE

Kathryn White
Illustrated by Vanessa Cabban

First published in Great Britain 2004
by Little Tiger Press

Text copyright © Kathryn White 2004
Illustrations copyright © Vanessa Cabban 2004

YUCK! THAT'S NOT A MONSTER!

Angela McAllister
Illustrated by Alison Edgson

First published in Great Britain 2010
by Little Tiger Press

Text copyright © Angela McAllister 2010
Illustrations copyright © Alison Edgson 2010

THE LITTLE LOST ROBIN

Elizabeth Baguley
Illustrated by Tina Macnaughton

First published in Great Britain 2007
by Little Tiger Press

Text copyright © Elizabeth Baguley 2007
Illustrations copyright © Tina Macnaughton 2007

LITTLE HONEY BEAR AND THE SMILEY MOON

Gillian Lobel
Illustrated by Tim Warnes

First published in Great Britain 2006
by Little Tiger Press

Text copyright © Gillian Lobel 2006
Illustrations copyright © Tim Warnes 2006
Visit Tim Warnes at www.ChapmanandWarnes.com